MASTERS OF THE UNIVERSE ™

NEW CHAMPIONS OF ETERNIA

Written by Jack C. Harris
Illustrated by Jeffrey Oh

A GOLDEN BOOK · NEW YORK
Western Publishing Company, Inc., Racine, Wisconsin 53404

The great halls of the Palace of Eternia rang with celebration as the Heroic Warriors returned from a victorious battle.

"We did it," cried Man-at-Arms. "We forced Skeletor and his army back across the borderlands to the dark side of the planet. Our warriors suffered only minor wounds."

His daughter, Teela, said, "I wish He-Man had come back to share in the celebration."

Man-at-Arms, Teela, and the other warriors were called before King Randor and Queen Marlena.

"We are proud of you," said King Randor, "but we are worried that Skeletor will soon launch another attack on the borderlands."

"We understand the danger," said Man-at-Arms. "We will get ready to return to the borderlands tomorrow."

Prince Adam pretended to have no interest in the battle plans. Only Man-at-Arms knew the prince was also He-Man, the most powerful man in the universe. He needed to keep the secret so that he could help protect Eternia.

At the same time, many miles away, on the dark side of Eternia, the evil lord Skeletor was raging at his followers. "Fools!" he screamed. "We have lost yet another battle to He-Man and his stupid kind. How long can I endure the likes of you?"

Just then, an evil light seemed to come into Skeletor's eyes. "Wait," he whispered. "There is a way to beat He-Man by using the blackest of black magic. It is the most dangerous magic I've ever used, but the situation is desperate."

Early the next morning, the heroes readied their vehicles for the long trek back to the borderlands.

"Be sure to pack extra battle gear," ordered Man-at-Arms.

After traveling all day, the tired heroes made camp.

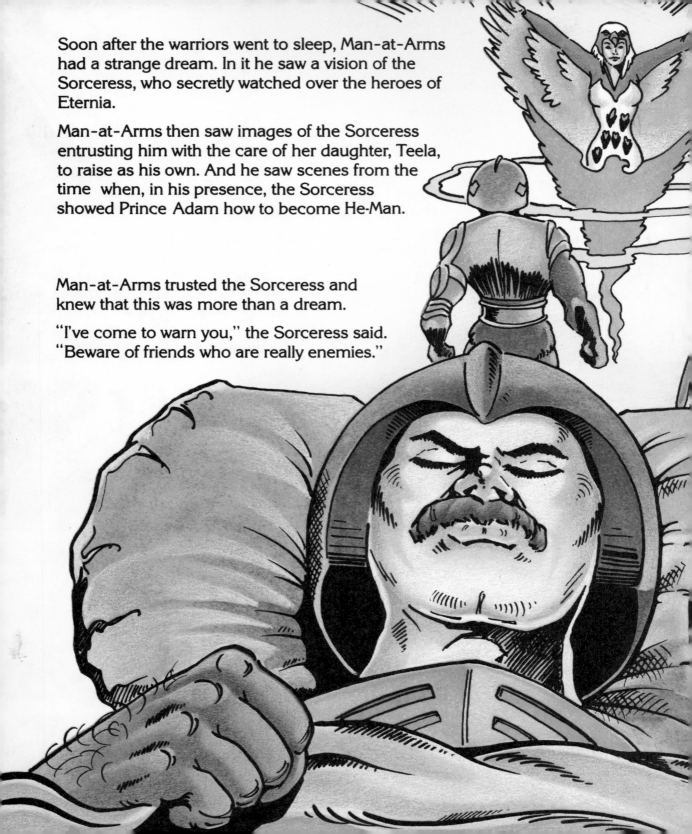

Soon after the warriors went to sleep, Man-at-Arms had a strange dream. In it he saw a vision of the Sorceress, who secretly watched over the heroes of Eternia.

Man-at-Arms then saw images of the Sorceress entrusting him with the care of her daughter, Teela, to raise as his own. And he saw scenes from the time when, in his presence, the Sorceress showed Prince Adam how to become He-Man.

Man-at-Arms trusted the Sorceress and knew that this was more than a dream.

"I've come to warn you," the Sorceress said. "Beware of friends who are really enemies."

At daybreak, the heroes greeted He-Man and Battle Cat as they joined the war party.

"What could the Sorceress have meant?" wondered Man-at-Arms. "Surely such friends as He-Man, Teela, and the others with us can be trusted."

Hours later, the heroes reached the cliffs along the edge of the dreaded borderlands. Across a barren field charged an army of Evil Warriors, led by Skeletor himself.

With loud battle cries, the forces of good once again faced the forces of evil.

"This is the final battle," snarled Skeletor, "for even if you defeat us, we shall win!"

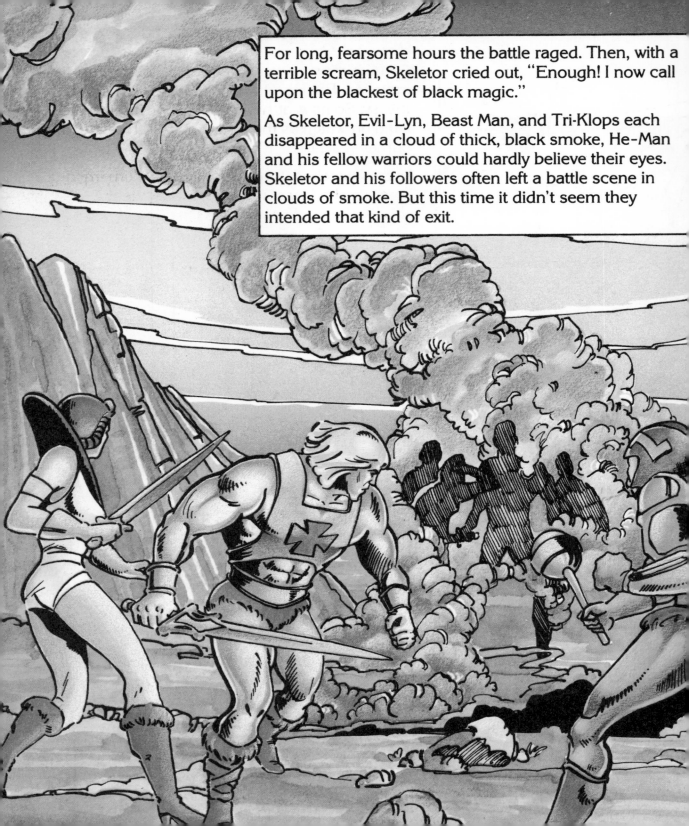

For long, fearsome hours the battle raged. Then, with a terrible scream, Skeletor cried out, "Enough! I now call upon the blackest of black magic."

As Skeletor, Evil-Lyn, Beast Man, and Tri-Klops each disappeared in a cloud of thick, black smoke, He-Man and his fellow warriors could hardly believe their eyes. Skeletor and his followers often left a battle scene in clouds of smoke. But this time it didn't seem they intended that kind of exit.

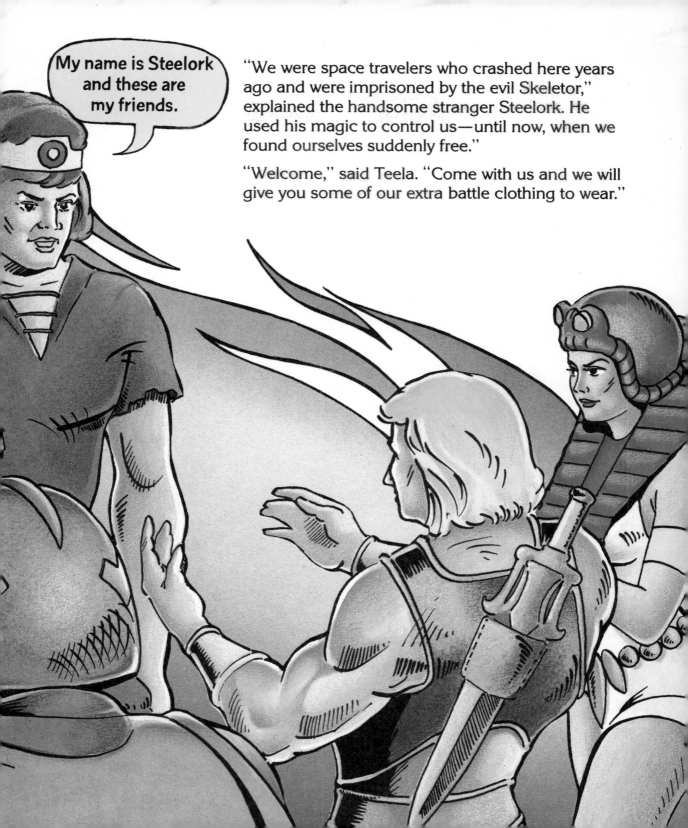

My name is Steelork and these are my friends.

"We were space travelers who crashed here years ago and were imprisoned by the evil Skeletor," explained the handsome stranger Steelork. He used his magic to control us—until now, when we found ourselves suddenly free."

"Welcome," said Teela. "Come with us and we will give you some of our extra battle clothing to wear."

Clothed and fed, the newcomers joined the heroes the next day in getting ready to return to the palace. As they broke camp, they were attacked by two of Beast Man's evil creatures, who had stayed near the battlefield. But the stranger called Abstanem was on them like a flash.

"What strength you have," Ram Man said to Abstanem.

"Yes," echoed Fisto.

On the long trip back to the Palace of Eternia, without warning, the stranger Potskril dived straight at He-Man.

Man-at-Arms told the others, "He was not attacking He-Man. He was saving him from that blade trap that Skeletor must have set before he destroyed himself."

Later, as the newcomers helped clear the path through the jungle, He-Man said to Man-at-Arms, "Something about these strangers bothers me."

"Yes," agreed Man-at-Arms. "In a dream the Sorceress warned me of friends who are really enemies."

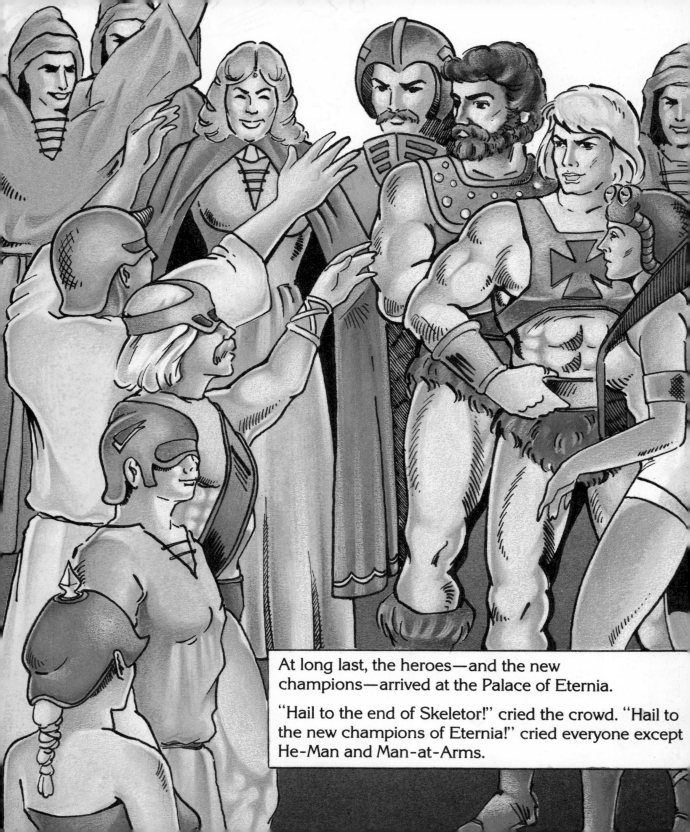

At long last, the heroes—and the new champions—arrived at the Palace of Eternia.

"Hail to the end of Skeletor!" cried the crowd. "Hail to the new champions of Eternia!" cried everyone except He-Man and Man-at-Arms.

When the cheering finally quieted, the king and queen stepped out onto the balcony.

"Hail to Queen Marlena," said Nyvelli as she knelt before the royal couple.

"Wait!" cried He-Man.

"Those new champions are cunning liars," said He-Man. "They claim they are strangers here, yet Nyvelli calls the queen by name. None of us has mentioned the name of either the king or queen. How is this possible?"

"I think I know," said the queen. "Listen to my story: I was not born on Eternia. Once I was a space pilot on a mission from a faraway planet. Due to the evil of my crew, we were lost in space and fell into a portal leading to this universe. When we crash-landed, I fell to this side of Eternia, where I was rescued by good King Randor, who later asked me to marry him.

"My crew fell to the dark side of Eternia and I never heard of them again—until, I think, this day!"

On the queen's order, the battle helmets of Nyvelli, Abstanem, and Potskril were removed so their faces could be seen.

"I thought I recognized your voices," the queen said. "And now I recognize your faces. You are really Evelyn Powers, a scientist from my crew; Biff Beastman, our technician; and Dr. Scope, also a scientist!"

"Yes!" cried the three as startling changes occurred. "But here on Eternia we joined with a great power and became Evil-Lyn, Beast Man, and Tri-Klops!"

"He-Man!" the queen's desperate voice rang out. "I know the sorcery that caused those changes—and the original ones, too. It's from the blackest underground pits of the planet....

"It belongs to...Skeletor!"

With that, Steelork reclaimed his true identity, amid a mass of smoke and flames.

He-Man shouted, "If this latest evil power of yours comes from the fiery center of Eternia, then it is that power I will tap to battle you!" And he plunged his sword into the ground.

Up from the center of Eternia, led by He-Man's magic Power Sword, a force of good emerged and banished the evil foes to the dark side of the planet.

Man-at-Arms felt the face of the Sorceress, within a cloud of white smoke, looking directly at him.

"We suspected something," explained He-Man and Man-at-Arms, "when these 'new champions' showed many of the same powers as the villains who we thought had been destroyed."

"It is lucky for all of us," said Queen Marlena with great relief, "that He-Man remained on guard."

At sunset, Man-at-Arms and Prince Adam were enjoying some quiet time.

"I was wary of our new 'friends' because of the Sorceress's warning," said Man-at-Arms, "and I am glad I did not trust appearances."

"Yes," said Prince Adam. "The Sorceress is a good friend."

He continued. "Today I learned that my parents are from two different worlds. And I know that the power of He-Man will battle for good for the sake of the heritage of both Eternia and that faraway planet."